Embrace the Beauty

Published by Dragonfly Hill Books, LLC

10 9 8 7 6 5 4 3 2 1
Embrace the Beauty

ISBN-13: 978-1-7327966-3-8

Library of Congress Control Number: 2018913232

Embrace the Beauty

A Collection of Poetry,

Flash Fiction, and Short Stories

C S C Shows

Dragonfly Hill Books, LLC

Dedication

For my family. You are my continued blessings and
constant reminders of how beautiful life can be.
Thank you for loving and believing in me.

Table of Contents

Introduction

"Let me embrace thee, sour adversity, for wise men say it is the wisest course." ~ William Shakespeare

"People have the natural capacity to affirm and embrace life in the most difficult of circumstances."
~ Rachel Naomi Remen

Change happens constantly, even when we try to ignore it or deny it. Some changes are so small that we barely notice them, such as the gradual changes in height of a child over months and years until suddenly that child looks more like an adult than like the child we remember. Other changes, like the death of a relative or a scary diagnosis from a doctor, can send us into a sudden tailspin.

Change is a sure thing, just like the constant turn of each season: cold spring rains turn to milder days, which give way to steamy summer all too soon, and the heat will vanish and inevitably turn cool with the falling leaves of autumn, temperatures dropping to frigid blasts of icy winds in winter. Just as each season turns to the next, so does the life of every person until it comes to an end.

How do you deal with the seasons of your life? Do you roll with whatever each day brings you, or do you spit and sputter and fight against the changing days?

Life has an interesting way of working itself out over time, and if you look closely enough, a beautiful and grand design emerges as you look back on the years of your life.

Maybe you have not seen it yet. Maybe you have not arrived to that season of life where images are clearer, where the pieces finally begin to fit, where the difficulties are disguised blessings, and where life is still mysterious but not chaotically so. Find the beauty hidden around you, search for it unceasingly, and when you recognize it, embrace the beauty in every season of your life.

Life is beautiful.

C S C Shows

Embrace the Beauty

Embrace the beauty of life's pieces,
Pieces thrown onto a table, a mixed up puzzle,
A puzzle that puzzles the mind and the heart.
With heart, embrace each day,
A day, only 24 hours, at a time,
Time will flow into tomorrow.
Tomorrow comes too soon,
And soon, you'll find that things fit into an order.
In order to see, step back, look at the whole picture.
The picture of your life is beautiful.

PART I – POETRY: Seasons of Life

SPRING

Sunday Morning Service

Folded hands in prayer,

Peppermint silence,

Humming hymns familiar

As the worn leather Bibles

In their leathery hands,

While stomachs grumble,

Souls mumble

For sustenance,

For succor,

For eternal rescue.

Precarious

Sandcastles crumble
Under the weight of the wave,
Weak under pressure.

Carousel Wish

A carousel spinning,
Mom and Dad wave,
Smiling delight with each pass round,
Mom and Dad talking,
They'll wave next time,
Look, here I come,
Her brows furrowed,
His shoulders slumped,
Familiar stance I ignore next pass,
Watch other parents waving, smiling,
Then dare a glance,
Mom alone, arms crossed,
Can I ride this carousel forever,
With its happy music and
Horses in fantastic colors?
Will they take me away
To a land as fantastic
If I keep going round forever?

What We Are Left With

A childhood fragmented by the Great Divide:
Anxiety and confusion ever-present
Where once naive confidence dwelled,
Innocence gone with our car packed in the night
To a haven hidden among the trees
Filled with the beat-down, the downtrodden,
And the nightmare-plagued troubled,
Those too afraid to sleep solo,
Slumbering in rows of single beds,
Mothers clutching children close,
Or grown women too afraid
To shut their eyes in a room alone.

We lived in fear there, too, for a while,
Two refugees in a sea of wringing hands and furrowed
    brows.
What if a man came knocking on the hidden door?
Or worse, came shooting through it?
This dread was constant, at least for a while,

A violent stranger with a shotgun blowing through the
    door,

Whose angry daddy or husband might find this place?

Mama folded herself around me each night,

Afraid I'd disappear while she slept.

Don't move.

Don't talk.

Don't disturb the others.

We slept, fully dressed, facing the bedroom door.

The bright hall light, always shining,

Would wake us if someone came in.

I clung to Little Lion, my nursery protector,

Dirty and small and beautiful,

Hidden deep in the toy box so no other damaged children
    would touch him,

Then stolen away, most prized of too few possessions,

Tucked in the cocoon Mama made of us each night,

My tears shed against his stitched up nose, hers against
    my hair,

Replaying Daddy yelling, tearing, breaking, ranting,
    raving,

Unhinged with anger too passionate to contain,

Frustration and curse words exploding throughout our house.

Don't get too comfortable; you can't stay here forever.

Blonde-haired Linda, with her second smile her husband made,

Too low, from ear to ear, became a familiar face among those that came and went.

How did she survive that, Mama?

She was proof that we women could endure anything.

Now, you must take courage and leave.

We packed our car again and ventured back into the world,

Carefully, watchful and wary, burdened and weary with fear.

Linda lived with us and taught me to braid,

To make my hair secure and beautiful,

But I was afraid her past would catch up with us

And was relieved when we parted ways, sad smiling woman.

Terror ebbed away in the following months and years,
Comfort settled in where life was calm.
Don't get too comfortable; you can't stay here forever.

Many years and the fresh sting of fears have passed,
But I'll never forget that a haven exists
For those who still knock at the door,
For mothers, and for tiny children,
Damaged and distrustful of the world.

Something Creeps

Something creeps,
It scuttles and hides,
You hear in the darkness,
Blind with eyes wide.
You open your mouth,
Ready to scream,
Shriek rising up,
Is this a bad dream?
Will you jump up,
Or will you stay?
Will you survive,
Or with life dearly pay?
You squeeze your eyes tight,
Throw covers over your head,
Somehow you'll be safe,
Still and quiet in this bed.
You shake until you fall asleep,
Dreaming dreams no child should keep,
A prisoner in REM deep.

Something creeps,
It scuttles and hides,
Waiting for the coming night,
Its pernicious time it bides.

Or so it seems,
To little girls with bad dreams.

Flowerchild

Flowers adorn you,
On your dress and in your hair,
Moving grace, beauty.

Games of Little Girls

Bubbles floating through the air,
Dandelion seeds blown with sweet breath,
Squeeze your eyes tight, make a wish,
Carried by the wind to who knows where,
Pulling flower petals, one by one,
He loves me, he loves me not,
Twisting apple stems to guess his name,
Ring Around the Rosie, Tag, Hide and Seek,
These are the games that little girls play.
Find the joy in such simple moments,
The silliness, the singing, the laughter,
Make wishes, play pretend, imagine,
Dance in the sprinkler, daydream.
Hold onto the innocence, tight as you can,
Childhood will be over in the wink of an eye.

Embrace the Beauty

SUMMER

Conflict of Expectation

You wanted a grown woman,
I was a naive girl.
You wanted a Marilyn,
I was a little sister.
You wanted too much,
I gave too much too soon.
You wanted me less,
I wanted you more.
You spread your arms to the world,
I only wanted to fall into them.
You wanted right now,
I needed forever.

How Brave You Are

How brave you are.
Summers born,
Think back,
Their eyes,
All lies,
Your eyes,
Big as the moon,
To be possessed of trust,
Veiled by dark rumors.
Let hope rise
Where none should exist.

Beauty to be,
Hands to do,
Lips to kiss,
Mind to see,
In another season
How one moves
In summer nights,

In dreams,

In decades since.

How brave you are

To be possessed of trust.

Wild

You wanted a rose,
Possessing striking reserve;
I'm a wildflower.

Hurricane

Hurricane force winds
Assail you with proof of it,
Iniquity monsoon.

Simple Girl

Torn blue jeans and sunflowers,
Red lipstick and wild hair,
Flying in the night air,
Girl, you don't know your power.
Sun kissed cheeks and silver rings,
Sipping on warm beer or cheap wine,
Dirt poor and doing just fine,
Happy with the simple things.
Always says grace at the table,
Don't dare underestimate her resolve,
Not a problem she can't solve,
Loves fiercely and smiles when she's able.

Rain Beats Oh

Rain drums on my heart,
Beats sound like sorrow,
Oh, lonely cadence.

Darkness

Inky blackness oozed out of every pore,
Until I abhorred myself,
In a tunnel with no point
Of light.

Hardly Love

You were hard to love,
Because you were never
The love of my life.
What was never meant to be,
Cannot be easy,
Cannot be right.
Meant to be
Sweeps you off your feet,
Takes your breath away,
Gives you dreams of a shining future.
You weren't any of that.

Fairytale

You thought you were
My everything,
Once upon a time.
You weren't
My Prince Charming.
You were
The Big, Bad Wolf,
Dressed in Lies
And Manipulation,
And villains don't win
In stories like mine.
My fairytale was amazing
Once you were off the page.

All Wrong

Being with you was never right,
Like pantomime in rhyme,
Like running on water,
Like snow in summer,
Like betting on time.
Thank God, I saw the light.

Mountains Meet Sky

Where mountains meet sky
In the smoky mists of dawn
Every morning,
I face other impossibilities,
Though never alone,
With my beautiful friend
I ride with purpose,
Mane of gold,
Muscles moving,
Heart bold,
The clop, clop of hooves a drum,
The cadence my song,
Matching my heartbeat,
Carries me when I'm weak,
When I'm sad, when I'm lonely,
Ever ready for new adventures
That emerge through the mists
Where mountains meet sky.

Impressions

You left an impression,
A handprint in dough,
Folded over and lost.
A wet footprint after a shower
That dissipates and vanishes.
A concert still in my head,
The roar of sound now absent.
But through absence, noticed.

You left an impression,
The lyrics of the song
Replaying on the tongue without thought,
Familiar tune, though altered in memory,
A sunset to the eye,
Momentarily blinded by the dazzle,
Fades to starry night,
A warm hand on my arm
Moved too soon,
The warmth cooling too quickly.

Oil paint on fingertips,
In cuticles, and under nails,
After the picture is finished.
The characters' voices,
Still talking in their familiar way,
After the book is ended.

You left an impression
That fades,
That changes with time,
What once was,
Transformed.

Run for Your Life

Running
This is my happy hour,
Place of peace,
Breathe in, exhale,
Feel the burn?
Got cramps?
Feel free to sing, wild thing.
Ponytails, crossroads, and sunshine.
Sights and sounds of summer,
Fall into autumn,
Bring on the cold.
Grab life on every corner,
Never fade.
It's all inside,
All that passion you hide,
Life pulses with every heartbeat,
With every deep breath and leg pump,
Eyes on the prize,
Beating my own expectations.

My secret, I sweat like a pig.

I swear like a sailor,

I get it done.

I'm a runner.

Ta-da! Wonder found.

What are you hungry for?

A truly natural progression,

If you think there's a problem,

Turning point: Running.

Be ready for anything, everything.

Run for your life,

Change a life,

Your life.

Love your heart

(Use it daily.)

Extraordinarily love,

Shown with each step forward,

Bring home something truly priceless,

The best new you has never looked better,

A sexy glow the old-fashioned way,

Recharged mind and body,
Live with momentum,
Love the life you live.

Your Song

Play me the notes in your head.
Are they discordant traffic honks and vrooms,
Are they stormy winds in trees,
Are they busy buzzing sweat bees,
Are they the hums of an efficient machine,
Are they water lapping the lake's edge,
Are they the whistle of a lonesome bird,
Are they hushed murmurs in a crowded room,
Or are they too quiet to hear?

Or do notes arise from your heartstrings instead?
Strumming notes soul-inspired,
Aching, loving, wanting desires,
Passionate fire, hurt, longing,
Regret, compassion, hope unending,
Notes with little reason and too much feeling.
Do you listen to these more,
These heart-tones of emotion?

Are you a head musician
Or a heart musician?
Or do the two play together
In a harmonic duet
Of notes and feeling?
How does your soulsong sound?
Is the key just right,
Is there perfect harmony,
Or do you need a good tuning?

Parade, Rest

Soldiers on parade
No cheers this year
No cheers for the soldiers
As they're paraded through town
Black instead of patriotic colors
Folded flags, not flying
At rest too young
Green beyond their battledress
Heads down, eyes on feet
Mothers crying tears
Wives holding little dears, confused
No cheers or bands playing
No cheers for the fallen
A march through town
A funeral march this year.
Valor buried with a salute and Taps.

AUTUMN

Autumn Song

Night arrives to the party
Too early, and stays too long,
Day tucks in for sleep,
Lazy, against chilly temps.
A bonfire crackles and pops,
Sparks dance in the sky
As if achieving stardom
Is their only goal.
Nature dresses in brightest colors
Before winter's dull-hued hibernation,
Red apples, orange pumpkins, yellow gourds,
Green leaves change color overnight,
Adorning the trees in brilliant leafy fabrics,
And winds whip and whistle around old house corners,
Like a man walking past a graveyard,
Whistling low to warn ghosts away,
As crispy leaves rattle like dry bones,
An autumn welcome song.

Built Tough

Love is an elaborate house,
Some built solid and tough
Of promises kept, plans made.
I'll huff, and I'll puff,
Will it all fall down?
Did you use trusty bricks
In the building of your future?
Or is it made from stinking, rotting straw,
To be scattered by violent breath,
And dirty words when times get tough?
Is it made of brittle sticks to be snapped
By stones thrown at weak spots?
Is your love built tough?

Epistle to Virgin Gorda

The sun sits high in the azure sky above the Caribbean
Sea.
Same sun that warms both places,
Though here hot and sticky, there temperate and salty.
I close my eyes against the assault of this sun,
And my mind wanders back to the Baths,
The place where I watched your scruffy smile blossom,
Sailboats and catamarans bobbing in glittering water
Just beyond the great boulders,
Those that had been beaten by winds of a thousand
hurricanes
But still sat, tenacious sunning natives,
Soft, wet sand between our toes,
Sidestepping driftwood bleached by the water and sun,
Skin soft and fragrant with cocoa butter lotion,
A stray crab with its pincers in the air,
Praising the beauty of this island paradise.

Now, I melt in the heat of a harsh sun,

Far away from the startling cacti and striking beaches of
  Virgin Gorda,
As I sip the remnants of a bottle of rum,
The Caribbean sun must be in a different mood,
Relaxed and happy, content with the sunbathers and
  yachts,
Gentle and hospitable to the beauty and color there,
While here, the sun beats down upon my shoulders,
The heat from it steals my oxygen and saps my energy,
It takes offense to the muted, uninspiring landscape,
With its brown patches, overgrown flower beds, and fire
  ant hills,
As though this place, less beautiful, must pay for its
  ugliness,
Vain, punishing star in a colorless sky.

As I melt in the heat of a harsh sun,
I write a letter to the elusive Devil's Bay
That watches the dark rises of Tortola in the distance:
Bring me back to the granite rocks that never move,
Erase a decade filled with tedium, struggle, and sorrow,

Clear water, pull me back into your cove with a foamy
    embrace,

Kiss my lips and hair with your salty waves,

Paradise, tickle my skin with your rainbow-hued fishes
    and warm breezes,

Hide me in your colorful grottos and under your tree-
    canopied paths,

Sun, blush my skin with your gentle rays,

Wink through passing clouds that promise a cool shower,

As I hold his hand and lazily snorkel among the coral and
    waves,

And forget the day, the year, the season of my life.

I curl the letter like a precious treasure map

And stuff it into my empty bottle,

I toss the bottle to the waves,

Hoping that it makes its way there soon,

Yet these waves lie to me, dust flies up,

Only heat waves, a mirage,

A dream of Caribbean waters,

Sand and grotto mazes,

Salt and vibrant fishes.

I sigh under the weight of the humid heat,

And I melt in the heat of a harsh sun.

Rainbow Grace

I arrived thinking of your arrival,
Not your departure.
I smiled thinking of your heartbeat,
But it was silent now.
I lay there open and vulnerable,
Life turned death inside me.
I suffered the loss of you
Before you were gone,
Before you were here.

I welcomed the absence of agony
As darkness descended, sweet amnesia ensued,
A reprieve from the pain,
But I woke up crying sheets of rain,
A storm let loose from oblivion,
And it stormed for days.
The loss lingered much longer than my tears,
Soggy and sullen skies threatened rain constantly,
I was woman defective,

Dejected childless mother,
Rejection of what was easy for others.

Nothing eased the edge of that loss
Until my rainbow appeared,
Beauty unfolded after the storm,
Alive and thriving, exuberant and sparkling,
Girls with sunny smiles brightened my days
As the sun peeked out
From the silver lining of heavy clouds.

Haibun of Healing

On a darkening day, the ultrasound machine was silent. No pulsing little flutter there anymore. Each word a startling clap of thunder that rumbles and shakes her heart.

"I'm sorry" and "This happens sometimes."

Clouds roll in too fast, and fat droplets fall like rain. After the black nothingness of anesthesia, a nothingness that came as a reprieve from the agony, and all hopes of motherhood are dashed, she is no longer expecting - expects nothing. No joy, no warmth, no further dreams of hair color and eye color and talents.

In the months that follow, she cringes every time she sees a mother with her pink, wiggling baby. Bitter tears wet her rough pillow at night as she holds onto nothing. She is broken, defective, unwomanly. Is she cursed? Had her years of selfishness, years of wanting an education and career over children, caused all of this hurt? Would this be her fate, to die childless, to be the nurturer of regret rather than descendants?

Another loss dashes hopes and rips her fragile heart into a million pieces of fluttering paper swept up and carried away by cruel winds in this terrible storm of life. All was darkness, nothingness too vast, an endless night of cloudy, starless skies. She wept away all her tears. What was life's purpose? To love and suffer? To struggle and pine?

She grits her teeth to bear the pain. Third time's the charm. Guttural cries turn to elated sighs as she holds her own pink, wiggling baby. A new day breaks through her blackest night.

Quiet beauty rare,
Elvish grin, strawberry hair,
Sweet, and Daddy's nose.

Sunshine twinkling smile,
Blue eyes flutter, butterfly wings.
She was worth the pain.

Last Child

The way your hair curls,
Cherub face, tiny fingers,
Pulls at my sad heart.

Climb into my lap,
Lay your head here for a while,
My last sweet baby.

Morning Glory, be
My light, my song, gentle dawn,
After dark nights, joy.

Tie Broken

How was I to know that last night
Would be the last time I'd nurse you,
Holding you safely in my arms
As you lay beside me,
In a way, still a part of me,
Still connected, so close to my heart,
Your tiny hand rubbing my stomach
Where once you resided safe,
Or patting my arm, entwined,
Only in those moments of quiet,
Of peaceful rest and sustenance,
No struggle to find your own feet
And make your own path,
How was I to know?

1+1

I tried to teach her simple math
In dirt on our carport floor.
One plus one like...
You plus your little sister equals...
She smiled and drew a heart,
Solving the problem,
Wise child.

Old-Fashioned Love

The youngins say that kissing is old-fashioned,
An outdated mating ritual,
Making out gone with the change of time,
Much like talking has.

They let their fingers
Communicate their desires
Over cell phone signal,
Then ignore each other
Face to face,
This poser love,
This love triangle
With two lonely people
And a cold phone screen,
How impersonal and odd.

I'd rather taste lips
Than bite my own
In sweet frustration,

I'd rather touch burning skin
Than caress a warm phone battery;
Give me antiquated mating rituals
Over new electronic love any day.

Vanity Extreme

Girls with darkened eyebrows,
Tattooed eyeliner plus cat-eye wings
And even magnetic lashes added,
Seven layers of gunk:
Primer, concealer, cream contour,
Foundation, powder contour, translucent powder,
And finally color on eyes, mouth, cheeks.
Covet thy neighbor's contours has become the new
  Commandment,
Fifty dollar palettes for colored pressed powders
In an array that would put a painter's palette to shame,
All layered and blended against skin
To alter the shape and shadow
Of their God-given faces.
Guess He wasn't artistic enough for you.
You spend hours a day learning all the tricks,
Watching videos on beauty tutorials,
Buying the latest products and brushes.
Lips, eyes, brows, part face, whole face,

Embrace the Beauty

Put your best fake face forward!
Add to it fake tans, hair rats, and booty enhancers,
Waist slimmers, hair extensions, and push-up bras,
Fake nails, collagen injections, and a pasted on smile.
Were you ever happy with any part of yourself?
If not, you can always turn to tech deception,
Photo software and apps with vanity filters -
No makeup, no problem!
Instant beauty found.
Except you look cartoonish, perfected,
Hidden behind obsessive beauty lies,
And you're only lying to yourself.
Your face, my dear, is an expensive canvas
That no one really buys.

Don't be a clown.
You are worth so much more
Than the mask you put on every day.

She Refused to Move or Fade

She refused to move or fade.
She defied the doom of her beauty,
While the winter of life lay beyond the hill.

Like the flowering old tree, stark and brilliant,
Its blossoms pink against the snow,
She refused to move or fade.

She stood vibrant and adamant,
Color and energy against gray,
She refused to move or fade.

Wild winds tangled her branches,
Tore at her leaves and buds.
She refused to move or fade.

She dug in and screamed in vain,
She gazed toward the glow of the sun.
She refused to move or fade.

She stood higher, braced against frigid gales,
She shook her curling branches.
She refused to move or fade.

While the winter of life lay beyond the hill,
And time pushed forward as it always does,
She refused to move or fade.

WINTER

Mississippi Mama

At fourteen, she left her Mississippi dirt-floor home
And took a bus to Memphis.
Working in a candy factory,
Living with a grown sister,
Living a grown life,
Innocence dissolved like peppermint,
Sugary and hot,
Sly words from sweet lips.
Child with child,
An unfortunate bastard,
The sweet life got hard again.

She sipped whiskey
Like sweet tea in the hot sun,
And found a moonshiner back in Mississippi,
Who took in her baggage
And gave her more children to bear,
More rows of cotton to pick,
More love, more heartache

Than she ever imagined
For one lifetime.

Real love came when her children were grown,
He gave her fifteen years
Of peace
And died by her in sleep,
Quiet heart attack that made her hurt daily.
She never trusted a man again.
Twenty-three more years she lived
Alone and free
From the possibility of heartache.
Alone, except for her children,
Which she bore through so much pain,
Who loved her hard-earned stoicism and strength.

She called to her mama
In the sharp pangs of her last days,
And her mama answered,
Guiding her home.

His Old Hands

(For my father, K.L.)
His old hands told a story
That his lips never spoke.

Ever steady,
Fists a short fuse,
Hands of judgment.

Building machines,
Family, and tradition,
Hands of purpose.

Cracked skin split,
Metal embedded within,
Hands of steel.

Folded in prayer,
Folded in mine,
Hands of devotion.

Deep wrinkles like rivers,
Tanned by hot days,
Hands of time.

Hands that held Ma Deuce in Vietnam.
Hands that picked Black-eyed-Susans and Daffodils for a
    girl.
Hands that clapped while grandchildren danced.
Hands that folded on his rising and falling chest in the
    morning sunshine.

His old hands told a story
That his lips never spoke.

Mama Amazing

(For my mother, Patsy)
You have amazed me through the years,
Settling for nothing, no matter the tears.
You love like no other person I've seen,
It's fierce and genuine and truly amazing.
You shine with the light of kindness, always a gentle hand,
Your compassion for others is without demand,
You find humor in tough situations, big or small,
And you held me up, tried to break every graceless fall.
These are the traits every mother should possess,
With you by me all my days, I have been truly blessed.

My Life is an Old Newspaper

My life is an old newspaper,

Black and white,

Easily smudged into gray,

Pages numbered,

The press wrinkled with use,

Days and years passing,

Like the flipping of pages

On a Sunday morning,

Features and highlights occasionally:

Excitement,

Death,

Prosperity,

Despair,

Hope,

Wisdom;

But mostly ordinary news

And opinion articles fill the pages,

Record of the mundane, insignificant occurrences

All chunked into sections,

Etched into rectangles of experience,
Recorded for posterity, this wisdom,
But largely forgotten over time,
Outdated medium pushed into a box,
Discarded with refuse,
Ruined by insects, rotting to dust,
Inevitably forgotten
In a world where too much trash
Mixes with bits of unnoticed treasure.

Fickle Muse

Muse, how you use me,
Flame of passion licks at me
Then is snuffed out, cold.

Patchwork

Her life was a patchwork quilt

Of experience:

Squares of pain,

Squares of happiness,

Squares of hope,

All pieced together by design,

Stitched together with intentions,

Sewn with colorful threads of dreams.

Care for You

I awake to your cries and angry fists,
Your simperings and your tears.
You've had more nightmares of angry men,
And I quiet your troubles and fears.

You don't quite remember where you are,
And I tell you that you're safe in bed.
You see your covers and familiar room
But can't get the images out of your head.

I murmur love into your hair,
I hug you to me tightly.
2 a.m. dream conversations,
This is our routine almost nightly.

You held me when nightmares frightened me,
And for you, I'll do the same.
You deserve the same sympathies since
In my childhood, my weakest moments, you came.

Your poor head is muddled with memories.
This misery I try to understand.
So Mom, I keep you close to me,
And I hold your soft, aged hand.

Her Memories Are Hers No More

Her memories are hers no more,
They bubble up and float away,
Her ship slips farther from shore.

The sun slants across the floor,
For a moment, she catches a ray,
Her memories are hers no more.

She grasps, then slips from her moor,
Waves crash and recede, heave her away,
Her ship slips farther from shore.

She wanders from door to door,
Does not know whether to go or to stay,
Her memories are hers no more.

Her mind too many sorrows bore,
Though she cannot remember them today,
Her ship slips farther from shore.

They think what a pity, how poor
To voyage through old age this way,
Her memories are hers no more.
Her ship slips farther from shore.

Another Day

Early in the morning
She woke after a fitful sleep.
Her bones creaked and groaned
Like the rusted hinges on the doors of her blue Ford truck.
She swung her feet over the side of the bed.
They wiggled into yellow slippers as familiar
As any other item in her bedroom.
She slowly made her way to the pink chair,
Pulled her robe around herself,
And edged over to the full length mirror
For probably the millionth time
Since she had first discovered vanity.

Her hair hung down her back in a loose braid,
Raven black, though now dull like coal.
Her fingers pushed against her cheeks.
Her thin lips almost blended in with the color of her skin.
Her eyes had not changed so much,
Though they were not as vibrant as before.

Her figure was gone, of course.

She turned this way and that,
Trying to get a glimpse of what she had once been.
She called out, "William, do I look so very different?"
Silence made her whirl around.
William was gone.
Had been for over a year.
How had she forgotten?

Another day would speed by
Like the cars out on the street,
Unrelenting hurriedness that spun her head.
She made breakfast,
Not because she was hungry,
But because she had always done so.
She stuffed cold grits, bacon, and biscuits
Into the refrigerator
And settled into the recliner.
So tired all the time now.
She felt like doing nothing,

Had nothing to do.
She listened to the outside noises
And nodded, so tired.

Her left side tickled with numbness.
William whispered to her,
She giggled at the hot breath in her ear.
Red wine from their picnic in the park
Trickled from the corner of her mouth
As her heart pounded with excitement.
She found herself lying in a field of lush grass.
She looked up at the sky, too bright.
Tears stung her eyes,
And she closed them.

Whispers

Blast of icy wind,
Your voice chills me to the bone,
Ghostly night whispers.

PART II – FLASH FICTION:

Moments of Change

Dust

Dust. It's everywhere. She breathes it in and blows it out. It has a smell she will never forget as long as she lives, the scent of ancient, tattered quilts forgotten in trunks. Dust covers her floors, her furniture, her skin. It makes purple look muted, like it isn't as bad as it feels.

It has been an exceptionally dry, hot summer. Burnt corn leaves on stunted stalks crackle in a slight breeze that moves the dust around. Her white dress, dulled by the dirt, pushes against her legs and then whips away from her. She walks across the worn wooden porch and settles down on the top step, a few small slivers of wood poking through her thin dress.

She'll never be able to do the man's work around this farm. No matter. Most of the crop is parched and wasted. The cracked earth juts up like broken, scaly brown skin. Maybe she can sell the farm since she is no longer a farmer's wife. She wants to see herself as something different than what she's been doing for so long. She can become whatever she wishes. She can work at the hair salon or maybe the post office. She can get secretarial work perhaps.

"Anything," she whispers into the hot air.

Dense, purple clouds move in quickly. Wind stirs more dust around, making little dust tornadoes that circle the barren front yard, entrancing her for a moment. Dust flies into her eyes, and she blinks it away. She throws up her small hand to shield her eyes.

A crack of thunder booms like his Remington, and she jumps. She laughs a little and pulls a strand of brown hair out of her squinted eyes that has escaped her bun. She hears and smells the rain before she sees or feels it, the wind teasing her nose with the perfume of rain.

From the west, a curtain of rain speeds toward her like the edge of the parted Red Sea, a gray wall as high as a mountain. She squeezes her eyes shut and waits. A torrent of rain drums her skin like hundreds of fingers, a liquid massage.

Pleasure rather than pain.

She doesn't move. The rain is warm but refreshing on her dry, tender skin. Her dress no longer slaps at her legs but clings to her like a second skin. Water trickles down her face, over her arms, across her legs, and pools at her toes, washing the dirt away. The sheets of rain make the world look completely gray as if the rest of it ceases to exist.

When the rain stops, the dust has disappeared. Colors are no longer muted and blurred. She sucks in a breath of humid air and her eyes widen. The vibrancy of the world startles her.

Stage Flight

There are 52 bones in the feet. Most are very small, but they all work together to sustain tremendous force placed on them daily.

Dancing hurts. It takes hours of work each day perfecting moves, jumping and landing, pounding the stage with the weight of the company on my feet. I wrap my ankles to protect the tendons as they stretch, propelling me to fly across the stage in grand jete or pas de chat. To fly, though. There is no better feeling.

Shots didn't work to curb the pain this time. Pain pills barely take off the edge. I flex my feet and wait to see what the doctors will say. In walks a doctor with x-rays that peek into my ankles and bore into my soul. Will I ever experience the rush of stage flight again?

He sighs, and I know the answer. Dreams of being a prima ballerina fly out the hospital window, and a tear drops onto my interlaced fingers, the knuckles white with more force put on tiny bones.

Only You

Gina drove along the narrow two-lane road at high speed, hands gripping the steering wheel. Something large flew past her windshield in the dark, but she didn't let off the gas pedal. Her body was tired, but adrenaline helped her focus.

She could outrun this. She was sure of it.

She had spent too much of her life spinning her wheels and going nowhere.

Gina grabbed a cigarette out of the open pack lying on her passenger seat beside her purse and gun. She lit it with trembling fingers, the light of the fire blinding her momentarily. She tapped the brakes.

The dark figure swooped down, just out of clear sight from her headlights.

"Not today," Gina declared. She took a big drag from her cigarette and felt a little calmer, the rush of nicotine subduing her jittery hands and calming her pounding heart a little. She pushed down further on the accelerator, taking curves in the road too fast.

Damn cancer.

She was 46. She still had so much life to live. Her kids were barely grown.

Gina glanced back at the man in the backseat, too afraid to take her eyes off the road too long. And too afraid of looking into his eyes; she feared she'd get lost in them and be gone forever.

The man in the backseat sat still, watching her politely. He sat with his hands folded in his lap over his black suit. His black eyes never blinked. His face was expressionless.

"Damn cancer," she said out loud this time so he could hear her. Had he heard her thoughts before? Maybe. Probably. But she felt like saying it aloud anyway. She took another drag of her cigarette. It wouldn't hurt anything now. It was too far advanced. Though she had taken painkillers only a few hours before, her stomach was a ball of fire.

"Time has come." His voice was flat, monotone, and she hated him for it.

"Screw you." Gina faked bravado, but tears stung her eyes and her lips twitched with sadness. Her vision blurred. She deserved more time. She had things to do. She wanted to hold her grandchildren someday born. She had never been to the ocean, and she ached for that experience now.

If she couldn't get more time, then maybe she'd end things her own way. That's why she had grabbed the gun when the man had shown up to her house. Or maybe she could shoot him. Could she kill him? She doubted it. When he had appeared in her backseat, just appeared there while she drove down the highway miles from her home, she knew she was dealing with something otherworldly.

The dark figure swooped down, this time coming into view, set on completing its mission. She saw black wings spanning at least eight feet and eyes that looked like distant stars. Not a bird but a blur of darkness between giant wings.

An angel of death.

"No!" she shrieked. Her heart thudded in her chest, and she wondered if she'd go of a heart attack instead.

Whatever was to be her end, he had made it clear that it would be now. And yet, she still held out hope that she could beat this.

"What can I do? What else do you want?" she bargained.

"Only you." His voice sounded like old papers fluttering. She strained to hear it.

Gina jumped when "Only You" began playing over her radio, which had been off. She wondered if he had a wicked sense of humor or if he was trying to comfort her with the old song she and her husband had danced to at their wedding.

Either way, her skin crawled, and she hit the off button in the dark with too much force, turning the volume up instead of off as she had intended. She punched the button again.

She realized that tears were streaming down her cheeks now.

How was she to face this moment alone? He had caught her unaware. She had been certain she had more time than this. She had no one to call on tonight.

Her two boys were in college. Her husband was working. She needed help during the day, so he worked nights while she slept to pay all the mounting medical bills this disease had caused.

She was alone in this.

She felt the heat of her cigarette burning into the filter between her fingers. She let off the gas pedal and flicked the butt through the open window, taking her eyes off the road only a split second.

When she looked back, all she could see was pine trees and tall grasses flying at her car. Then, she felt the jarring impact.

Gina hit the copse of pines at 67 miles per hour.

Gina found herself above the mess of metal and glass and pine. The flying angel of death gripped her effortlessly. She stopped struggling.

She saw the man open the back door of her totaled SUV, straighten his black tie and coat, and walk into the night as she was taken up farther and farther into the sky.

Gina's body lay mangled in the front seat until the accident was found the next morning.

Cause of death: fractured skull due to blunt impact of head as a consequence of collision of motor vehicle.

Time of death: approximately 11 p.m.

Just the Wind

The campus church bells rang out nine deep, slow chimes. Helen had lost track of time working on her homework in the campus coffee shop after her late class. She pulled her coat closer to her body as she trudged across campus to the back parking lot where she had parked earlier. Helen began to get the creeping feeling that someone was following her. Her scalp tingled, and her stomach and hands felt heavy. She had learned to trust her instincts. She picked up her pace, trying to dismiss her fears as she went.

Clouds had moved in that evening, and they blocked out the half-full moon, leaving most of the campus in darkness except for the occasional inadequate orange circle from a street light that only made the shadows everywhere else look darker. With the clouds came gusts of wind that swept past Helen's ears, muffling sounds of a passing car, the bark of a dog somewhere in the distance, the footsteps of a maniacal serial killer hell-bent on cutting up unsuspecting college women.

Helen shuddered and shook her head at her own gruesome imagination as she rounded the corner of a dark building and looked back over her shoulder. She saw no one. She stopped for a moment to see if she could hear anything. No use. The wind battered the dry leaves on the trees, sending some of them cascading down around her. She couldn't hear anyone behind her.

Helen pulled the set of keys out of her coat pocket, gripping the solid car key like a shank in her palm. It wasn't much but was at least something. It didn't give her much comfort, but she rubbed her thumb against the fob in nervous agitation. Helen began walking again, this time chiding herself for being silly. Still, she looked back again.

A big man in a dark coat, his head dipped low against the wind, had just rounded the corner and was gaining on her. He held something in his hand.

She almost screamed but swallowed the sound. The deafening wind would make her screams useless anyway.

She turned and pumped her legs forward, praying the guy wouldn't attack her. She envisioned her bruised, blood-soaked body being discovered the next morning, maybe even by one of her professors or a classmate.

Tears began to run down her cheeks. A hand grabbed her arm. Her own hands, small as they were, came up instinctively in defense. She swiped the key near his face.

"Hey!" The man shielded himself. "You left your cell phone on the table at The Blue Spoon."

Helen gave a nervous laugh as he handed it to her and walked away. She felt ridiculous.

"Thanks," Helen called to his back as an afterthought. Her body was still pumping adrenaline, her heart thudding so hard she thought she might have a heart attack, even after the threat was gone. Shaking, she walked to her car, thankful that this had not been her last night alive.

As silly as she felt about almost attacking the man trying to help her, Helen knew what kind of world in which she lived. It was better to be safe than sorry.

Balloons for Bee

Amanda gathered the balloons by their strings and pulled them out of her SUV. She was early. No one had arrived. She stood in the field, looking into the murky water of the pond.

The ground was level, perfect for a party. Mom didn't like having them here because it could be dangerous. Bee insisted her last few parties were here, though, because she loved to fish.

Clouds covered the sky, making the water appear darker. A mist rose from the water after an unseasonably cold night. Amanda was glad she had chosen a sweater this morning.

Her little sister, Beatrice, who everyone had always called Bee, very fitting for such an active little girl, would love this rainbow of balloons. Amanda smiled thinking of her sister's bright grin and the way it lit up her green eyes. She still looked at the pond, though she saw her sweet sister's face instead.

Where was her dad with the tables and chairs? Where was Mom with the chocolate cake with sprinkles and candy letters and all the gifts? Amanda gripped the balloons tightly so they wouldn't escape her grasp.

Bee was born in autumn, so the grass was brown and crunchy. It would have been better if Bee had been born in the spring like Amanda had, when the weather is gorgeous, everything is in bloom, and the sun warms her skin. Bee loved autumn, though. She loved jumping in leaves, picking pumpkins at the patch on Miller Road, dressing up in wild costumes for Halloween, and telling ghost stories at midnight around the fire pit in the backyard. She was such a fun eight year old.

Had Amanda gotten the time wrong? She glanced at her watch. She looked around, but no one else had arrived while she daydreamed. Her eyes again rested on the still water of the pond, the mists rising from the water like wispy ghosts. The sun peeked through clouds, making the ghosts disappear.

She heard an engine in the distance. Finally, someone was arriving. It was her father in his pickup. When had he gotten a red one? Where was the blue one?

He stepped out of his truck, his brow gathered in worry. He wore the same old cap, but he looked older. He moved slowly, too. He seemed changed.

He stopped beside her and looked out at the pond.

"Ghosts," Amanda whispered.

"It wasn't your fault."

"What wasn't?" she asked.

"Don't make me say it," her father warned.

Amanda looked at him, confused.

Her father stared out at the water instead of looking at her. "You were only a year older. I hate finding you here on this day. I don't come here anymore on purpose."

"Is the party somewhere else?" Amanda gripped the balloons tighter, too tightly.

"No," the old man sighed. "No party." He pulled his cap off, scratched his spiky gray hair with the brim, and replaced his cap.

No party? Oh, that's right. Amanda frowned. She turned back to the water.

Dad turned to walk back to his truck. "Go on back home. Or come to the house. Your mother is still in bed, but you can have some coffee."

It was a hollow invitation. He cranked up his truck, backed out, and drove back through the field to the gravel road, a cloud of orange dirt billowing up behind his pickup.

She turned her eyes back to the pond. This time, she saw Bee in the water. She stepped forward to call out to her. Bee was still, her long hair floating out from her head. She was pale, no sweet smile, though her face was serene. Amanda felt her heart break again. She let tears fall without wiping them away, blurring her vision until she only saw colors. She blinked her tears away.

Amanda realized she had let loose the bunch of balloons she had been holding for Bee. They separated and rose higher into the air, so high that they became specks before they drifted over trees and out of sight. She turned her eyes back to the pond. No Bee, only still water.

"Happy birthday, Bee. See you next year," Amanda whispered.

Beware the Mergoddess: A Mythic Prose Poem

Your modern mermaids are ridiculous caricatures,
Quintessence of goodwill and fantastical romance,
Guiding sailors through storms and around rocks or
    falling in love,
Anderson's childish fairy tale only a snippet of truth.
Homer cast a more honest hue with his hypnotizing
    Sirens of the ocean deep,
Or the legends of vicious Sirenas of the Philippines,
Singing sex and sending seamen to their watery graves.
What actually lies in the deeps is sinister and powerful,
Vengeful and lustful goddess of the ocean,
Epitome of the desires and fickleness of woman,
The most beautiful creature ever to behold,
And no mortal man can escape her hands if she ever seizes
    him.

I will tell you the true tale of the mermaid, as you call her,

Stolen away to the deep to escape.

The Mergoddess, known throughout antiquity

As the immortal love goddess turned ocean queen,

Once known as Atargatis by the Assyrians,

As Aphrodite by the Greeks, created from murder and
seafoam,

Lover of Poseidon, who gave her a home,

A sea-palace fit for a goddess,

When threats to Mount Olympus became tiresome

And she returned to the sea from which she was born,

Escaping terrible Typhon, monster-god of Gaia,

Giant serpent-haired, red-eyed fiend,

Turning her back on the passions and wars of man,

And fleeing a loveless marriage to Hephaestus, this once
Goddess of Love,

Far from the threats, turmoil, and sorrows of life with
humans and gods,

Making a palace deep within the Mariana Trench,

Away from temptations that caused too much agony,

Nearly forgotten as new religions took hold of the lands.

Tangaroa, the Polynesian sea-god, allows her dominion
over the deep Pacific

And grants her permission to rise to the waves

On stormy nights to do her sinister bidding,

And there she rules to this day, with lust and murder in
mind,

In her dark, watery kingdom in the Sirena Deep.

In the deepest reaches of the ocean, where no Sonar can
quite creep,

In the hidden, coldest blackness, she waits for her
hopeless prey,

Ascending at night only when the clouds blow in with a
storm

And cover the blinding light of the pale moon and hide the
dazzling starlight.

Missing the touch of men, those she scorns yet yearns for
constantly,

She seeks them as they bob and toss on the ocean in ships,

She feels their manliness pulling at her core,

She smells them through the salty waters,

She swims far under them, twisting in the currents,

Waiting for her chance to be seen, to be touched,

To be adored and lusted for, and when she can stand the throb no longer,

She begs Poseidon to shake the ocean and bring the waves,

She summons Fa'atiu to raise the winds

And beckons the Anemoi to bring on the storms,

She gnashes her teeth and pulls at her flowing hair until she can emerge,

Anticipating each time that she can feel hot skin,

Kissing, sucking, tearing the flesh of sinewy seamen and salty sailors.

She calls her siren cry, and the winds pick up, dark clouds rolling across the sky,

Lightning splits the darkness, then a crack of thunder as the waves rise,

And she moves closer to the ship that slips across the sea.

Her eyes dazzling diamonds, her lips dripping rubies,

Her skin phosphorescent in the stormy night, glowing like
the moon itself.

He catches sight of the mesmerizing Mergoddess as he
struggles with the ship,

Every atom of his body attracted to her, pulling toward
her,

He heeds no warnings of mermaids or sirens, though he
has been told,

And into the churning water he is compelled.

She inhales his smell, touches his oily soft hair,

Rubs her naked skin across his, reveling in the warmth
she misses.

Her fingers caress and press and curl around his heated
flesh,

She licks and tastes and nibbles and gnaws

Straight to the bone, as he screams in pleasure,

Pain so wonderfully sensual that no mortal man can pull
away,

He wraps his muscular, tanned legs around her,

She pulls him to her breasts, where no heart beats,

She snatches him under and dives deep

Until his lungs explode and he writhes no more.

She descends, unquenched, unsatisfied, frustrated, and
unfulfilled,

To her shadowy subterranean palace,

Ornamented with pearls and sailors' bones,

To wait for another nocturnal treasure hunt.

This is the Mergoddess's ritual, her curse

For residing in the deep so long

And for loving men too much.

PART III – SHORT STORIES:

Transformation of Perspective

The Motherhood Club

Charlotte hated babies. Okay, that wasn't fair. She didn't hate them, particularly. She didn't like the idea of babies and what they turned women into. Independent, amazing women seemed to lose all sense of self after having children. She had grown up with no siblings or young cousins, so she really didn't have any experience with babies. Maybe fear of the unknown was what made her dislike them. She never understood the fascination many females felt toward the squirming, chubby little humans. They screamed and understood nothing but selfishness and left a trail of messes behind them.

Charlotte knew motherhood was a necessary part of life. She was glad it wasn't a part of her life.

She was thankful that the woman who had come in with a baby strapped to her back in a carrier only stayed long enough to pick up her Macchiato and blueberry scone and exit. The smell of poop or the shrill screams that normally came with them made Charlotte cringe when a baby would enter the coffeehouse with a parent.

Charlotte wiped down the tiger oak counter, satisfied that the beautiful golden wood gleamed in the amber light of the coffeehouse where she had made her home away from home for the past four years of college. She loved working there and would miss it when she graduated in a few months. She had never felt that way about a job before. Coffee made people happy. So did the pastries. She saw smiles every day, and it felt rewarding.

Right now, a cold March wind blew around the shop windows with a low howl, sending new blossoms scattering from the early-budding green trees along the sidewalk. The coffeehouse was cozy, so she ignored the frigid weather outside and returned to the textbook she had been reading and highlighting. It was only 9 a.m., but she was already hungry for lunch. She rung up a cinnamon roll, put the cash in the drawer, and nibbled on the pastry as she studied.

The morning coffee crowd rush had passed, and only a few customers came in here and there. When a group of women came through the door, Charlotte realized she had forgotten that it was Tuesday morning.

In they walked, the Zmombies, Charlotte had nicknamed this motherhood club, a group of women who wore impressively dark circles under their eyes, trudged almost senselessly under the weight of diaper bags, baby carriers, and too little sleep, and sought coffee and brains, or at least adult conversation. The Chipped Cup was their favorite brunch spot on Tuesdays, and at least a few of the women always had small children with them, usually sniffling with a cold or strep or some other contagion.

These women were like talking automatons of nurturing as they wiped snotty noses, changed putrid diapers, pulled out leaking boobs to feed them, and sipped lattes as if nothing out of the ordinary were happening, all the while talking about Montessori, Pump and Dump, Linea Negra, and Push Presents, all of which were like another language to Charlotte.

Still, she envied their staunch resolve to be there for each other every week despite the obvious trouble it was to get themselves out the door and into the coffeehouse in a semi-presentable state. These women had found their tribe, something Charlotte had never been able to do.

Sure, she had had plenty of good friends over the years, but somehow, they never seemed to be constant. One best friend dissolved into another, a line of friends loved fiercely and then gone, either because they'd had a falling out or because of a gradual growing apart.

Yet, even Charlotte knew these women's names and most of their kids' names, too.

Bonnie, a red-lipped and rosy-cheeked eight month old in a boutique outfit that was probably more expensive than the clothes Charlotte wore, grabbed her mother's $200 shades and flung them. They clattered and then slid across the floor, resting at the front door.

"Your turn," Jimmy said. "My shift is over in a few minutes." He grinned a wicked smile, and she swatted his arm with a cloth.

Charlotte left Jimmy behind the counter gathering up trash to take outside before he left. With a ticket book in hand, she walked over to the group of women as they settled into their seats. She picked up the shades for Kelly, Bonnie's mother, and handed them back to her.

One baby, a fussy newborn named Henry whose mother complained about constantly for suffering colic, was already starting to cry, and Charlotte noticed that a customer who had been sipping his coffee and working on his computer abruptly began packing up to leave. She understood his frustration. She would be getting no more studying done for the next hour or so. Charlotte didn't know exactly what colic was, but it must be hell for the mother to have to endure day in and day out.

"Good morning," Charlotte greeted them. Only a few of them actually looked up at her, not preoccupied by children and diaper bags or their phones. "May I take your order? We have delicious cinnamon rolls and chocolate chip scones this morning." God, a chocolate chip scone sounded amazing right now. At this rate, she'd have to spend the whole afternoon on the treadmill to burn the gross amount of calories she would eat today. She wondered if she was anemic. She felt off.

The woman closest to her, Suzanne, looked up as if surprised that Charlotte had appeared beside her. "I bet Tommy would love a chocolate chip scone, Charlotte." Suzanne motioned to a little boy who was pulling napkins from a dispenser. Tommy had gotten more and more destructive over the winter. Charlotte guessed he didn't get enough time outside because of the cold weather. Or maybe little boys were just like that.

"I bet." Charlotte tried to smile. Just what a mischievous two year old needed - more sugar. This woman must be a glutton for punishment. "Got it down. What would you like?"

"Green tea. I'm still nursing," said Suzanne with a smile while another woman nodded in approval, "so no caffeine for me."

Charlotte scribbled on the ticket, trying to hide that she had widened her eyes at this comment. Nursing is natural and healthy. Nursing is natural and healthy. Nursing...She couldn't get the visual out of her head of this child with a mouthful of teeth latched onto this woman's breast. Didn't that hurt? She was trying not to be judgy here. She smiled again, trying to atone for her thoughts. She planned to breastfeed. Well, maybe. If she ever decided to have children. She had seen some of these moms over the months nurse a child in the coffeehouse, and they always looked deeply connected with their children. She also noticed that it was an instant way to quiet shrill cries. That had to be a good motivator to breastfeed.

One mom in the group, a slim blonde that usually didn't have her kids with her, was sporting a new baby bump, Charlotte noticed, as the woman rubbed her hand over her tight blouse. She looked pale and disheveled, which was a stark contrast to the way she was normally more put together and bouncy than the rest. "I need something with ginger in it. I've already puked twice this morning. Bring me a bagel, too. Plain. And a water. Which reminds me, I've got to go pee again."

Once Charlotte jotted down the orders, she went back behind the counter, working to the steady chatter of moms and children. She brought over children's orders first because she knew that food would keep them pacified for a little while. Besides, the moms never got to eat or drink anything until kids had been taken care of. Maybe Charlotte knew more about children than she realized.

Charlotte was only halfway through her shift, but she was dragging today. When the Zmombies finally shuffled out, she wiped down the tables and swept up crumbs and spilled coffee and tea, thankful for the tips she pocketed while cleaning up the huge mess left behind. She sagged against the counter, ready to go home for a nap after work. She was glad she had no afternoon classes today. She nibbled on a chocolate chip scone and highlighted her textbook. She placed her elbow on the counter and her head in her palm, trying to concentrate on the text, but her eyes grew heavy.

"Excuse me."

Charlotte's eyes fluttered open, and an older man, a homeless gentleman who came in some days for a warm cup of coffee, stood in front of her.

"I'm so sorry." How had she fallen asleep? And for how long? "Ready for a cup of coffee, Mr. Greene?"

"Yes, ma'am. Thank you." As he turned to sit down at a table and wait for his charity treat, Charlotte caught a whiff of body odor that made her stomach turn. There was no homeless shelter around here, so it was normal that Mr. Greene didn't always smell too pleasant, probably cleaning up as best he could in public restrooms. Also, he often took liberties with the dumpsters around town, selling, using, or eating whatever he could salvage. Today, Charlotte had to turn away, the smell catching her breath. She made him a large cup of coffee and put a few scones left over from yesterday into a paper bag and went over to where he sat.

"Bless you." His toothless smile was genuine, and she felt bad trying to hold her breath. "You look different today, Ms. Charlotte. Thank you kindly for the food."

"Yes, sir. Keep warm, now."

When she was sure he was down the street, she sprayed Lysol into the air and cleaned the table where he had sat to try to eliminate the smell he had left behind.

Charlotte didn't know if it was the mixture of Lysol and stench, her suspected anemia, or a stomach virus coming on, but her mouth began to water and her hands and cheeks tingled, and before she knew it, she was running to the restroom to vomit.

Charlotte was so glad no customers had been in the coffeehouse to witness her dash to wretch over a toilet. She stood up in the stall, her hands shaking and the smell of vomit in her nostrils, and she grimaced. She did not need a stomach virus. She had a really important midterm to take tomorrow morning and another one on Friday. She couldn't be laid up in bed sick. She washed her hands and rinsed her mouth and face with water from the restroom sink and went back out to the counter.

An elderly couple had come in and were standing at the counter looking up at the menu on the wall.

"Hello. May I take your order?" Charlotte asked. She pumped a bit of hand sanitizer on her hands and rubbed it in, hoping that if this was a stomach virus, she wouldn't get anyone else sick today.

"I think I'd like a caramel cappuccino. My husband wants a tall hazelnut coffee, same thing every time." The old woman smiled, her eyes crinkling deeply at the corners, as the man laid a ten dollar bill on the counter and shuffled to a table in the corner to read his paper. Charlotte poured the hazelnut coffee, the nutty smell relaxing her churning stomach a bit, and got the woman her change from the cash drawer.

"I'll bring your cappuccino over to you."

As Charlotte handed the woman the money, the woman grasped her hand and enveloped it in her own smooth, cool grip. "Sweetheart, crackers and clear soda always helped me with morning sickness." Taking the money from her, she patted Charlotte's hand and turned to join her husband.

Charlotte stood planted to the spot. She snorted. "No, I'm not..." She frowned and turned, remembering the cappuccino, and as she let the espresso machine do its magic, she stood in silence, counting up the days since her last period.

It had been six weeks, so that was over two weeks late.

She hadn't noticed, but she had been so busy with school lately. This semester had been pretty stressful.

Stress! She grinned. She bet it was stress that had delayed her period.

Deep down, she knew this wasn't true, and her smile faded. Not for two weeks. Everything added up to pregnancy: her moodiness, her exhaustion, her insatiable hunger, and now her nausea. Tears stung her eyes, and she blinked them away. Charlotte would get a pregnancy test on the way home to confirm it, but she knew what the test would say.

In a daze, she delivered the cappuccino to the old woman and went back behind the counter, staring at her open textbook but seeing nothing written on the page. She would be a mother? She knew nothing about kids.

How would her fiancé react to this news? Adam shared her desire to live selfishly unfettered by children, at least for a while. They were both so young. She wouldn't even graduate for a few more months, and he had a year left of grad school. They were planning on a big camping and hiking adventure in Grand Teton in a few months. It was her graduation present from Adam. She guessed she would be trading in her hiking boots and camping gear for baby equipment. She sighed, her shoulders sagging.

How would she find a job while pregnant once she did graduate? She imagined dressing for job interviews with her bulging belly sticking out and shaking hands with potential employers at job interviews she would be sure never to get.

Ugh, this was terrible timing. Awful, dumb luck. She took a soda from the cooler and sipped on the sweet, bubbly liquid. It did help a little.

Charlotte scrubbed at the already clean and shining counter. She had wanted a beautiful wedding and a fun honeymoon. She had wanted to work in her career for several years before even thinking about a family. What she wanted was flying right out the window now. She felt nauseous all over again. She watched the clock, hoping her relief would show up soon.

Charlotte toyed with the idea of a baby as she cleaned. Would it be a boy or girl? She imagined buying sweet little socks and warm onesies for next winter. She imagined

Adam holding their child, and she felt a little better about the situation. What would their child look like? She tried to imagine. Would their child have his deep brown eyes or her icy blue ones? What would her child's talents be? She thought the baby might have her musical talents and Adam's mathematical intelligence. Maybe the child would be a wonderful baker like Adam's mother or really handy with woodworking like Charlotte's father. She smiled to herself. Maybe it wouldn't be so bad.

Charlotte wiped down the stainless steel espresso machine. As she caught sight of her disheveled hair from the vomiting escapade in the restroom and the sickly paleness of her skin in the reflection of the stainless steel, it hit her. She would turn into a Zmombie soon.

Charlotte would be the one walking in with a milk-soaked piece of cereal stuck in her hair and snot on her shirt where a child had rubbed a runny nose across her blouse. She would be the one with dark circles under her eyes and crooked eyeliner. Or no makeup at all.

Still, she could also imagine being the mother who dressed up her children in sweet outfits and took pictures that celebrated age milestones and holidays. She could imagine singing to the baby as it cooed and then drifted off to sleep on her chest. It couldn't all be bad, or women wouldn't be mothers.

None of her friends had children yet, and the idea frightened her that she might be doing this alone.

Charlotte had a feeling she would find herself wandering back to The Chipped Cup before too long on Tuesday mornings to find some camaraderie in the misery and miracles of motherhood.

Job Hazards

What's about the easiest job a 26 year old man can have where there isn't much responsibility and virtually no danger? Short order cook. And that's exactly why Jake had taken the gig. It was supposed to be easy and safe, anyway.

Jake entered the diner through the back door. The stench of old grease and raw meat assaulted his nostrils, made him catch his breath. Had the freezer broken again, or was that faint putrid smell still lingering from the last time? Maybe it was just his growing displeasure for the smell of raw meat. He clocked in and grabbed a blue apron from the wall before heading to the kitchen. Another short-order cook, Lionel, who had been working at Mary's Diner for the last decade, perked up when he saw Jake enter the kitchen. He flipped two burgers and handed Jake the spatula.

"You're five minutes late, Jake-o." Lionel reached for the pack of cigarettes and the lighter he kept stuffed in the pocket of his apron, which was speckled with old grease splatters. "Thought I was gonna chew my arm off itchin' for a smoke." Lionel had mean nicotine fits since Mary had stopped him from smoking in the kitchen several years back.

"Traffic," Jake mumbled.

"Traffic, my ass," Lionel threw over his shoulder as he exited to the back alley. Jake looked through the kitchen, past the counter, and out the window that faced Main Street. Not a car in sight.

It would be suppertime soon. The daylight was beginning to fade, and the streetlights blinked on here and there along the street outside the diner. The nine-to-fivers would be getting off work any minute. Mary rarely let two cooks work at the same time. She was too cheap. But for two hours around lunch and supper, she had the cook leaving and the cook coming in work together to cover the extra customers. Mary herself usually cooked breakfast in the mornings. Because Mary's was the only one of three sit-down restaurants in Kitterton, the rush hours could get hectic in a moment's notice with only one cook in the kitchen.

Jake loathed working with other cooks, preferring to have his space and do things his own way. Not that Lionel was such a bad guy. But it riled Jake to be told in which order to put dressings on a cheeseburger. When Lionel was in the kitchen, Jake had to do things his way. He was the senior man. Only three shakes of the salt shaker on the fries, crap like that. Lionel mouthed about his seniority if Jake tried to give him lip about it. Besides, Lionel kind of smelled. Jake wondered if he showered regularly or if it was just old man smell.

Jake smacked the bell at the window, and Tamara, a cute redhead with an athletic build, grabbed the two burgers and fries and took them to a couple of teenage girls in a booth. Tamara was a senior in high school herself. She wore a red Mary's Main Street Diner t-shirt, tied tight at the waist to show off her slim midsection and a little skin. The girl was a quick learner about making good tips, apparently. Mary, who was pretty business savvy, had hired Tamara although she had no experience waiting tables. A cute, young face brought in more customers.

Jake threw some more frozen fries into the basket and lowered them into the boiling grease. He would have to clean up quickly tonight if he wanted to make it to his band's gig. He didn't want to go to a gig smelling like stale grease. Over the cigarette smoke in the bar, it probably wouldn't make a difference, though.

He picked up the fry basket, the fries a little too brown and crispy, and dumped them into the fry bin to salt them down. Five shakes, just for old Lionel. He stole one and popped it into his mouth. He hadn't eaten anything before coming to work. He had actually been late because he had been out job hunting. Lately, he felt so restless there. He couldn't be a cook forever, like old Lionel. Two years was too long. When women asked him what he did for a living, he'd always tell them that he played guitar for Lake of Fire, named after his favorite song by Nirvana, but never told them about the diner.

"Hey, Jake. Want a drink?"

Jake jerked his head up. He hadn't heard Tamara come back from serving the girls at the booth, who were giggling at the Elvis song playing faintly over the speakers. Mary had decorated the diner in 1950s and 60s music nostalgia, complete with menu selections like the Chubby Checker Double Decker Club Sandwich, Great Balls of Fire Chili, and Nat King Cole Slaw. Most young people thought it was corny, but Jake liked it. He had grown up listening to his parents play records from the era and watching old Elvis, Gidget, and Jerry Lewis movies with his mom. Most kids didn't even know who those icons were anymore.

"Sure," Jake said. He watched Tamara as she fixed him a fountain drink, her ponytail swinging back and forth as she bounced with youthful energy. Tamara handed it to Jake through the order window. Her fingernails were painted blue, he noticed. Drinks were the only thing Mary allowed the employees to have for free.

"When are you playing again?" Tamara cradled her jaw in her hand, furiously chewing the bubble gum she had just popped into her mouth. She seemed so young when she did that, even though she was already eighteen. He wondered if she was planning to come see the band.

"Tonight, at the Green Door. Gotta get out of here in a hurry to make it." Jake sipped on his drink as Tamara stared at him. When he looked up, she looked away.

"I'll be here until closing," Tamara stated, "so get the kitchen pretty well cleaned up, and I'll take care of mopping the floors tonight." She cast her eyes down at the brown linoleum floor and picked at her nail polish.

"Great. Thanks, Tamara." Jake winked at her when he caught her eye and began chopping a head of lettuce when she turned away to check on customers. He hummed a new tune his band had been working on that week. It was a slow piece that picked up about midway through. Freddie, the lead singer of the band and Jake's best friend since elementary school, had written it a week earlier, and most of their practices had been centered on it.

Jake smiled to himself thinking about how sweet Tamara could be. Why weren't grown women like that more often? He leaned out the order window to see her better. She was looking at a textbook. "Let me take you out sometime as thanks for the extra work you're taking on tonight for me."

Tamara looked up from her homework, a slight frown on her face. "No, that's all right, Jake. It's no big deal."

Jake ducked back into the kitchen and winced. Ouch! Maybe he had read her wrong. Or maybe it was just wishful thinking.

Lionel, who had just walked back in, snorted behind Jake. "Ah, the sting of rejection. You could get in trouble with that one."

Jake kept his voice below the music. "Nah, she's legal. Maybe she just ain't into older guys."

"Maybe she just ain't into you, Jake-o. Ever think of that?"

Jake ignored Lionel, hoping Tamara hadn't heard him, and walked to the back to start cleaning up what was left of the pile of dishes from the lunch crowd that Lionel hadn't gotten to yet. Tamara appeared at the window with a call-in order, which Lionel got busy working on. Jake flipped on the radio by the large stainless-steel pit of a sink and dunked his hands into the hot water. He realized the radio was set to a local country station from Harrisburg County, the next county over. He really didn't like that type of music, but his hands were already wet, so he left it alone. After the slow, mopey song went off, a local news reporter came on.

"This is Rebecca Friedman with your WLOK Quick News Update. Police are still investigating a convenience store robbery in Harrisburg County that took place last Monday. Police have stated that the convenience store did not have proper surveillance equipment and have not made a positive ID of the perpetrators. More WLOK news on the hour." Jake rarely ever went to Harrisburg County other than to play an occasional gig. He doubted he knew anyone involved. More strains of whiny steel guitar and long drawls of sadness slid out of the radio speakers as Jake finished up the pile of dishes.

The rush never came that night. Sometimes it didn't in a small town. It just depended on the impulses of the townsfolk. Once Lionel had finished his shift and gone home to sit in a cloud of smoky nicotine bliss, Jake relaxed and ran the kitchen at his own pace. Because the night was slow, he found plenty of chances to talk to Tamara. He didn't know much about her. She had only been working there about a month. She worked part-time, only a few nights per week.

At around 8:15 p.m., the bell over the door jingled. Tamara looked up from her math homework. Jake had just come from the back, where he was restocking supplies onto the shelves, huge cans of jalapenos, various containers of seasonings, and boxes filled with napkins and straws. He carried a tray of refilled salt and pepper shakers for Tamara to put on the tables to replace those that had gotten low. The new customer was obviously pregnant from the size of her bulging belly, in her mid-twenties, maybe a little younger than Jake, and looked like she'd seen better days. She had her hair pulled back into a messy ponytail and had a faint scowl on her face. She seemed familiar to Jake, but he couldn't remember if she'd been in the diner before. She shuffled in and sat at the counter near where Tamara was doing her homework. Tamara erased something on her notebook paper and blew bits of eraser off the page. Jake liked the way her lips puckered out when she did that.

"Hi." Tamara smiled, popped her gum, and handed the woman a menu. "What would you like to drink?"

The woman surveyed the menu and chose iced tea. While Tamara filled her glass, the woman glanced at Jake, who was watching from the kitchen. He began wiping down his work area with a soapy dishrag.

Tamara turned around and placed the tea in front of the woman. "Let me know when you're ready to order."

"Thanks." The woman looked hungrily at the menu, devouring the words with her eyes as though the descriptions were tangible. Finally, she said, "I'll have the...I'm a Believer Triple Cheeseburger with bacon, the Four Seasons spicy fries, and can you put some extra pickles and onions on the side, please?" She smiled shyly.

"Of course," Tamara replied, jotting down the order. She slapped the ticket down in front of Jake, who had already thrown the hamburger patties on the grill. He added a new batch of spicy fries to the oil. He went to the back to get more bacon out of the freezer. When he returned, Tamara and the woman were chatting about her pregnancy.

"I get cravings for greasy food just about every night. I know it's not good for me, but when a craving hits, it's hard to deny. All I can think about is french fries." The woman laughed, and Tamara smiled. The woman made small circles with her hand over the top of her stomach while she sipped from her glass of tea.

"Caroline, that's Jake. He's a cook by day and a rocker by night."

Caroline grinned as Jake played a few seconds of air guitar on his spatula. Tamara rolled her eyes and shook her head. Caroline took another sip of her tea and then added a couple of packets of sugar to it. She stirred the sugar with her straw, and the granules settled to the bottom of the glass. "What are you studying?" asked Caroline.

"Oh, Algebra II. It's like a foreign language to me. I'm terrible at math," confessed Tamara. She shifted to the other foot and crossed her arms.

"Be glad you're finishing up school. I wasn't so smart. I hated high school, and no one could talk me out of quitting."

"I graduate in just a few months."

"I got married before I was even supposed to graduate. We're not together anymore." Tamara, Jake, and even Caroline herself looked down at her stomach, but no one said anything. The sound of the sizzling hamburger patties and bacon and strains of the guitar from "House of the Rising Sun" filled the silence.

The jingle of the bell again signaled the new arrival. Kenneth Jenkins, a night security guard at Adams Machine Works, strode in and picked out a seat at the counter near the kitchen window.

"Whatcha know, Kenny?" Jake called out while finishing up Caroline's order. He also filled a dessert plate with dill pickle slices and stout onion and set it in the window beside the burger and fries. "Order up!"

Tamara had already poured Kenny a cup of black coffee to help him stay awake. He claimed that he could stand a spoon straight up in Mary's coffee.

"Cold tonight. I could see my breath when I got out of the truck. It ought to be warm this late in the spring," Kenny grumbled. "Blackberry winter, I guess." He added a little sugar to his coffee and took a sip. It always surprised Jake that Kenny could drink steaming coffee right out of the pot and not scald his mouth and throat with it. He never added water or ice or even blew on it a little, just gulped it on down as soon as it was placed before him.

Tamara had gone back to studying while Caroline devoured her greasy meal. She had a smile on her face every time she looked up, chewing her food quickly before getting another bite.

"How's the band doing?" Kenny asked in between careful sips.

"All right." Jake leaned forward, propping his elbows on the order counter. "We're playing in town tonight."

"Rough crowd at that bar you play at, or used to be in my day."

"Still is, I guess."

Kenny raised his eyebrows and then furrowed them into a frown that his face now wore. "You young ones. You never realize danger, even when it's staring you in the face. Someday, you'll think, 'Why did I ever put myself in that kind of position?'"

"Or I might think, 'That's where it all started on my journey to fame.' Your job could get just as dangerous as mine," Jake pointed out.

"Yeah, but it's doubtful. Who's really going to hold me up for a welding machine? Besides, I don't think that compares to twenty-some-odd drunks busting beer bottles and chairs over each other's heads. Tamara, can I get a piece of that pie?" Kenny pointed toward the peach pie on the counter.

Tamara uncovered it, cut him a piece, and slid it onto a plate. "Want some ice cream, too?"

"Better not, hon. Got to watch my figure." He patted his belly, which stuck out farther than Caroline's. Caroline had polished off her entire meal except for a few rings of raw onion and sat sipping her tea while listening to Kenny and Jake talk.

"The Green Door isn't that bad. We see a few getting rowdy, we just play a slow song or two. They even keep a bouncer there now. It's not so bad. Anyway, I'd play music anywhere."

"How long has your band been together?" Caroline asked.

"About four years," Jake replied proudly. Most bands never made it that long. It was usually girlfriends or booze and drugs that broke them up.

"Ever think of taking it to the city?" Caroline asked.

"We actually play some gigs occasionally up in Brownsville and Harrisburg, but we never have gotten into the recording studio to record our demo we've been talking about. It's pretty expensive. Maybe it'll happen one day. Seems like every time we have the money for it, something comes up."

"Maybe I'll come see you play sometime. After the bun's out of the oven, of course." Caroline smiled.

"Don't get him started on his music," Tamara said. "I've heard more equipment talk and music lingo in the last few weeks than I'll probably hear for the rest of my life." She went back down the counter toward the door, where her Algebra book still lay open.

"Tamara looks so much like my Jane when she was a girl. Coming in here and seeing her takes me back forty years." Kenny looked wistfully at her and then studied the contents of his coffee cup. He finished up his pie and looked at his watch. "I better get out of here early tonight. Pete said he needed to leave a few minutes early, so I guess I better go relieve him." Kenny stood up, turned up his coffee, took a five out of his wallet, and put it down beside his plate.

"See you, Kenny." Jake waved to the old man.

Kenny put on his Kitterton Security Company cap, tipped his hat as he walked by the two ladies, and exited the diner, the bell above the door jingling its goodbye.

"I can't believe how hungry I am tonight." Caroline looked out the front window and back at the pie on the counter.

"Want something else?" Tamara cleared Caroline's plates.

"I guess maybe I could eat some of the peach pie. And some vanilla ice cream, too." Caroline smiled sheepishly.

"Wow, you do have an appetite. Being pregnant must get pretty expensive." While Tamara was getting Caroline's dessert, Caroline scooted off her stool and waddled to the restroom. The bell above the door jingled again. Jake looked up, half-expecting Kenny to be coming back in because he had forgotten something. Instead, a tall, skinny kid in dark clothes walked in. The oversized dark gray hoodie he had on covered most of his face. His dark denim jeans seemed dirty in the bright light of the diner. He walked quickly to a booth near the back and slid into it.

Caroline came out of the restroom, glanced down at the guy sitting bent over in the booth, and went back to her seat at the counter. Tamara strolled over to the booth, greeted the new arrival, and handed him a menu. As Caroline ate her dessert, she locked from Jake to Tamara to the guy in the booth. No one said a word, but Jake didn't go back to his work, either. Jake guessed the guy made everyone uneasy.

What happened next made time seem out of joint. Things slowed down half-time and sped up double at the same moment.

The guy threw his menu down with a plastic pop that made Caroline and Tamara jump. He jumped up from the booth, and he strode toward the counter. Jake gripped the edge of the order window, wondering what this guy was up to. It hadn't dawned on him what was happening yet.

The guy had his hands tucked into the big pockets of his hoodie and pushed a pointed object through the material. He stood about ten feet behind and to the right of Caroline, placing himself where he could see both the girls and Jake. Jake, Tamara, and Caroline stared at the guy.

"Don't be stupid, now," the guy sputtered. He seemed revved up, like he was on uppers or maybe just a load of adrenaline. The three in the diner looked at the guy with a mixture of dawning recognition, disbelief, and fear. Caroline dropped her spoon into the already melting vanilla ice cream, and it splattered across the counter and onto her stretchy tan and red shirt. The noise scratched

138

his raw nerves, and he twitched a little. "All right, girl. Get into the register. I want what's in there."

Tamara stood with her pencil in her hand, her mouth slightly agape. She shut it and turned toward the cash register, which faced the door at the end of the counter. Jake couldn't see her face, but he could see her hands shaking as she hit various buttons, trying to open the register though sense had left her in the terror of the moment.

All the while, Jake was trying to clearly see the guy's face beyond the shadows of the hood. If he was on drugs, Jake reasoned, the guy could do something irrational and would most certainly be unstoppable by just him. He had seen Cops. Guys on Meth and other stuff could fight off sometimes three cops at once. He looked at the pointed object in his pocket, trying to determine if it really was a gun. The cash register finally slid open, and Tamara grabbed the bills out of the drawer, slapping them on the counter with a shaking hand and stepped back.

The guy looked at the bills and looked back at Jake. He squinted his dark eyes. Realizing he couldn't get the money and leave and keep his eye on Jake at the same time, he yelled, "Get your ass out here. I want to keep my eye on you." He motioned with a wave of the object in his pocket. "Don't try to be a hero." His voice was low and smooth and threatening.

Jake moved toward the door that lead from the kitchen into the dining room. As he was moving, he began to wonder what the guy might do. He stopped as he rounded the counter. Why hadn't he thought to stick a kitchen knife somewhere? He hadn't thought fast enough. What idiot brings a knife to a gunfight, though?

"Move it, asshole," the guy impatiently instructed. He motioned for Jake to come around the counter. Holding his hands up about chest-high, Jake walked toward Caroline.

"Sit down beside this one," he demanded, looking at Caroline. Jake sat between Caroline and the robber, trying to at least shield her with his body. The guy turned back to Tamara. "Now, I want you to get the key that's hidden behind the daily specials menu on the wall and open the safe under the rug at your feet." He glanced at the door and front windows. "Hurry up!"

Jake wondered how he knew about that. He must have been casing the diner for days, probably learning their routines and seeing where Mary got the money from to go make deposits each night at closing time. He probably also knew that Mary carried a pistol with her.

Jake was sweating despite the cold of the night. He didn't want to die. He may not have done a lot with his life, but it was his, and he liked it well enough.

Tamara followed the guy's directions, pulling several hundreds and a stack of twenties out of the safe. She laid those on the counter beside the money she had gotten out of the register. Her bottom lip began to quiver. She looked like she'd burst into tears at any moment. Caroline looked at her dessert and placed her hand on her stomach. Jake had been the only one to get even a somewhat decent look at the guy's face. Maybe he could remember enough to help the police, if he survived.

"Get a paper bag out and put the money inside. Hurry up."

Caroline's breathing was coming quicker, like she was beginning to hyperventilate. Her body rocked back and forth as she breathed. The thief looked over his shoulder to make sure no one was coming up the sidewalk. Tamara stuffed the money into the bag as fast as she could and sat it down on the counter. She took a step back, not looking up.

"Frankie, don't hurt 'em." Caroline had gotten up. Tamara looked up at her and blinked in confusion.

"You know this guy?" Jake whispered. Had this thug used Caroline to case the restaurant? Were they in on it together?

"Shut up. I told you to come in and get something to eat first, not become best friends with the victims."

Victims? Oh God, the guy was going to kill him and Tamara. What reason did he have for killing them? Couldn't he just take the money and leave them the hell alone? A dozen different scenarios played out in Jake's mind at lightning speed. Too many possibilities, too many options. He couldn't think straight. He looked at Tamara, hoping it would refocus him. She looked wide-eyed and wild, her nose flared and her jaw set.

"Can't you just take the money and get out of here?" Jake boldly asked. Could he even reason with a person so reckless? "What do we have to do with it?" Frankie's arm moved fast in Jake's peripheral vision, and before he could move, Jake felt a sharp crack against the side of his skull from the gun Frankie hid in his pocket. Frankie hit him so hard that it knocked him off the red vinyl stool. He lay there, seeing shocks of light in his vision but didn't black out.

"Stop it, Frankie," pleaded Caroline. She pulled on Frankie's sleeve. "You said you wouldn't hurt anybody. Let's take the money and get out of here."

"What's with you taking all night to get a burger?" Frankie frowned and looked over his shoulder again.

"I had to wait for the security guard to leave in case he had a weapon. Besides, I was hungry. I'm growing a human."

"I don't like the look this guy's giving me." Frankie waved his gun around. "I think he's gonna try something. I'm thinking we should tie them up."

"Let's just go. Before that security guard comes back or someone gets hurt. We've done some bad things, but murder won't be one of 'em."

Lost in their conversation, they didn't notice Tamara easing down behind them, her eyes wide and riveted to their figures.

"Let's get out of the state and never look back. Bring up the baby in a good place with a new start. We have plenty of money now." Caroline pulled on Frankie's arm again, and Frankie looked down at Caroline's stomach.

They didn't see Tamara bringing up the big Louisville Slugger. Jake shut his eyes tightly, sure that at any second, he'd hear Frankie shoot Tamara. Imagining it was agonizing enough. He couldn't see it really happen.

By the time Tamara had pulled the bat back behind her shoulder, Frankie turned, noticing movement, and swung around just in time to see Tamara swing as hard as she could with a guttural growl of anger.

She made contact with his face. Jake heard the sickening crack of bat hitting bone. The force of the blow knocked Frankie off his feet and sent him backwards several feet. His face blossomed a red flower of blood, and he lay on the floor motionless.

Caroline covered her eyes and screamed. Tamara stood posed with the bat pulled up behind her shoulder again as though she expected Frankie to rise up like some horror movie monster. Jake laid on the floor, dizzy from the smell of blood, the pounding of his head, the shouting repetition of "La Bamba" from the speakers, and the sound of Caroline's maddening shrieks.

Somehow amidst the dissonance, Jake heard the bell over the door jingle. Mary filled the doorway, the night deposit bag dropping from her fingers.

"What in God's name happened here?"

***

Jake walked into Mary's Diner, the bell jingling over his head as he paused to let his eyes adjust to the dim light. Tamara squealed. "Jake!" She came out from behind the counter to hug him. "I haven't seen you in a while. Where have you been hiding?" Her cheeks were speckled with light freckles from the summer sun.

"Lake of Fire has been booking some pretty good gigs lately. Apparently, grunge rock is on the rise again around here. Or so the young folks tell me."

"Pfft, the young folks. Sit down and stay a while, old man."

It surprised him that he could still see blood that was no longer there. He couldn't believe how brave Tamara had been that night.

"Have you had to use your slugger lately?" He sat down on a stool, his back to the area with the phantom blood.

"Nah." She popped her gum and moved around to the back of the counter. "Once word got out that I can swing a bat, the bad guys have pretty much left us alone. Mary even gave me a raise," she grinned. "Says I'm a badass and worth keeping around." She looked at him sheepishly, and he felt his cheeks grow hot. He hadn't been fired, but how could he stay there after that night?

Tamara grabbed the pot and poured him a cup of coffee. "Sorry, did you want that?" She laughed. "It's such a habit. I never knew so many people drank coffee all throughout the day."

"It's fine." He sipped the bitter, black coffee. "We were lucky Mary kept a bat down there."

"And we were lucky I was the best hitter on the high school girls' softball team."

"That, too."

Tamara smiled and then a look of gloom crossed her face. "I don't blame you for leaving, ya know."

Jake waved her comment away. "I hated being a cook anyway." Tamara leaned down, her elbow on the counter and her chin resting in her palm. He looked into her green eyes, which had so much understanding, far too much for a girl of eighteen, and said, "I guess it's nuts that I feel safer as a security guard."

"Well, you know what Kenny says. 'Who wants to steal a welding machine?'"

"Yeah." Jake laughed. Kenny had done him a solid by getting him on with Kitterton Security. He sat at the counter sipping his coffee for a while, listening to the familiar sizzle of food frying on the griddle, people chattering and clinking silverware on dishes, and the jingle of the bell, which made him look toward the door every single time someone went through it.

Before he left, Tamara came over to ask him if he wanted anything else. He pulled a few dollars out of his wallet and laid them on the counter for his coffee. "Come by and see me play some night. Maybe you can be my bodyguard at the Green Door. Bring that bat with you."

"Haha." Tamara rolled her eyes. "Are you ever going to let me live that down?" She smiled a little and leaned back, watching him.

"Saved by a girl? No way. I am glad that you smashed his face in. They had robbed a bunch of places before they got to us. The police think he wasn't doing it for the money anymore but for the thrill. Who knows how far he would have gone?"

Tamara looked down at her hands. She said, "Yeah, who knows?"

A customer hailed Tamara for his check, so Jake said goodbye to her and walked out the door of the diner, flicking the bell with his finger overhead as he exited. He was a little ashamed that he didn't react well to the place. He couldn't get the image of Frankie's smashed face and the sound of Caroline screaming over and over out of his mind. Or the feeling of dread and hopelessness he had felt in those moments before Tamara had acted.

The security job was different than the job at the diner. He liked the sense of control he felt as he walked the familiar paths of one of KSC's client companies. He liked that he knew the dark corners and what was in them. He liked that even if there was danger up ahead, he was prepared for it instead of being blindsided in a supposedly safe job.

Jake knew the risks he took at the bars, and he knew the risks of a security job. They seemed a lot less insidious than the uncertainty and vulnerability of a wide open oldies diner on the corner of Main Street.

Visit my website for updates about upcoming projects, release dates, and special giveaways, and sign up for my newsletter at http://bit.ly/cscshows

Please take a few minutes to leave a review on Amazon, Goodreads, or your favorite retailer's website. Reviews are so helpful for authors. We rely on and appreciate your honest feedback.

You may contact me at cscshowsauthor@gmail.com.

Instagram: @csshows
Twitter: @CyrenaShows